WHAT ... DY

D0381246

BOOKS BY PETER PEREIRA

The Lost Twin
Saying the World
What's Written on the Body

WHAT'S WRITTEN ON THE BODY

PETER PEREIRA

COPPER CANYON PRESS

PORT TOWNSEND, WASHINGTON

Cover art: Images © iStockphoto.com / Michael Blackburn, Les Byerley, Peter Chen, Jordan Chesbrough, Sandy Jones, Paul Senyszya, Carolina K. Smith.

Copper Canyon Press is in residence at Fort Worden State Park in Port Townsend, Washington, under the auspices of Centrum Foundation. Centrum is a gathering place for artists and creative thinkers from around the world, students of all ages and backgrounds, and audiences seeking extraordinary cultural enrichment.

LIBRARY OF CONGRESS CATALOGING-IN-PUBLICATION DATA
Pereira, Peter, 1959–
  What's written on the body / Peter Pereira.
    p. cm.
  ISBN-13: 978-1-55659-252-2 (pbk. : alk. paper)
1. Body, Human—Poetry. 2. Physicians—Poetry.
3. Medicine—Poetry. 4. Gay men—Poetry. I. Title.

PS3616.E74W47 2007
811'.6—dc22

2006031167

98765432 FIRST PRINTING

COPPER CANYON PRESS
Post Office Box 271
Port Townsend, Washington 98368
www.coppercanyonpress.org

ACKNOWLEDGMENTS

I am grateful to the editors of the following magazines, newspapers, and anthologies, where some of these poems first appeared.

Art Access: "Holy Shit," "Reconsidering the Seven." *Bloom:* "Twenty Years after His Passing, My Father Appears to Us in Chicago, at Bobby Chinn's Crab & Oyster House, in the Guise of Our Waiter, Ramon." *Blue Fifth Review:* "Body Talk," "The Push," "Y." *Caffeine Destiny:* "Anagrammer II," "Channeling Madge," "Think or Swim." *Dermanities:* "Scald," "Beauty Mark." *Digerati:* "Turbidophilia," "The Cruciverbalist," "Damn Fag," "Holy Shit," "Burning the Nests," "Perfect Pitch," "Mount Baker in August," "Butterfly Bush," "What the Skin Cutter Feels." *Good Times Weekly* (Santa Cruz): "Dream of the Cancer Cure," "Perfect Pitch." *In Posse Review:* "Holy Shit." *Journal of the American Medical Association:* "Case History: Persephone," "What's Written on the Body," "Tremor." *Literary Salt:* "October Journal," "Onionmania," "Night-blooming Cereus," "The Corpse Flower." *The Long Journey: Contemporary Northwest Poets:* "Anagrammer," "The Devil's Dictionary of Medical Terms." *Manzanita Quarterly:* "Aeschylus in the Park," "Night Walk," "Precip," "What the Skin Cutter Feels." *New England Review:* "Nursemaid's Elbow." *Northwest Gay and Lesbian Reader:* "Ganymede to Zeus," "Ravenna at Dusk." *180 More: Extraordinary Poems for Every Day* (Billy Collins, ed.): "Anagrammer." *Poetry:* "Anagrammer," "Turbidophilia." *PoetsWest:* "Attending Rounds," "Hearts." *Prairie Schooner:* "After *The Pillow Book*," "Damn Fag," "Inattentive," "Missing *e*," "Serafina," "Tic Douloureaux," "The Garden Buddha." *Rock & Sling:* "Dante Reconsiders *Paradise*," "The Judas Tree." *Seattle Review:* "Aesop's Dog." *The Sound Close In: Poems from the Third Skagit River Poetry Festival:* "Breathing Lesson." *Spinning Words into Gold:* "Turning Straw into Gold."

Three Candles: "Burning the Nests," "Butterfly Bush," "Perfect Pitch." *USA Today Weekend:* "Weekend Healing." *Virginia Quarterly Review:* "The Cruciverbalist," "Turning Straw into Gold." *West Wind Review:* "The Scholar's Garden." *Willow Springs:* "Crossing the Pear."

Thank you to fellow writers and first readers of many of these poems: Sharon Bryan, Martha Clarkson, T Clear, Jeff Crandall, Kathleen Flenniken, Linda Greenmun, Kathryn Hunt, Charles Jensen, Beth Kruse, Jared Leising, Rebecca Loudon, Ted McMahon, Rosanne Olsen, Susan Rich, Ron Starr, and Gary Winans. Thank you to Michael Wiegers and Joseph Bednarik for their support of my work. Finally, thanks to Copper Canyon Press for a Residency at the Vermont Studio Center, where many of these poems were written.

CONTENTS

for Dean Allan

I. ANAGRAMMER

Anagrammer

If you believe in the magic of language,
then *Elvis* really *Lives*
and *Princess Diana* foretold *I end as car spin.*

If you believe the letters themselves
contain a power within them,
then you understand
what makes *outside tedious,*
how *desperation* becomes *a rope ends it.*

The circular logic that allows *senator* to become *treason,*
and *treason* to become *atoners.*

That *eleven plus two* is *twelve plus one,*
and an *admirer* is also *married.*

That if you could just rearrange things the right way
you'd find your true life,
the right path, the answer to your questions:
you'd understand how *the Titanic*
turns into *that ice tin,*
and *debit card* becomes *bad credit.*

How *listen* is the same as *silent,*
and not one letter separates *stained* from *sainted.*

Turbidophilia

love of trouble

Pleasure, ease, contentment: a bore.
Where's the rub? The snafu? The glorious glitch?
Tiff. Tizzy. Tumult. To-do. Remember:
no itch, no fuss: no pearls to string.

Feud, fit, flap, flurry.
Hoopla. Imbroglio. Rhubarb. Pickle.
What good's a shampoo without lather?
Soup unstirred? Wedding without a row?

I want spasm, spat, squabble, stink.
Brouhaha. Boondoggle. Conniption. Clash.
Calm's as good as dead: a plum-pit.
Give me ruckus, rowdy-dow, ruffle, snit.

Tête-à-tête

My heart is like a singing bird
whose nest has caught on fire.
A fire started by a lit cigarette,
an oyster bisque. *Ponies have nothing*
to do with peonies, he opines.
His finger slicked with saliva,
circling the rim of a wineglass.
I ask him to open his shirt.
How our lives evolve and revolve.
If eros is a form of erosion, then
I'm feeling a little ob(li)vious tonight.
Like someone who talks with both hands.

Possessed by Words

He thinks it all began with
"Begin the Beguine" — those pleats
of petals like Ecclesiastes. Now,
whether it's hearsay or heresy, who's
to say? Whether it unites or unties,
this word illness leads to silliness,
then stillness. How reverse the spell?
He remembers the mother
smearing her breast milk
into the baby's eyes. The doing
of one thing the undoing of another.
How they said it was too late,
by the time they got to the hospital —
it was *too late,* the infection
was *florid:* meaning, like flowers.

"Man Convicted of Killing Wife Second Time"

The Seattle Times, April 2, 2002

What fractured syntax! And hard to say
which is worse: that he'd hack her to pieces
in the bathtub as the children slept,
or that ten years later he's convinced enough
of his innocence, to drag himself to trial again.

Either way, the mother of these kids
is still gripping a lily, her name bolded
across headlines, killed all over again —
hatchet wounds fresh as the crime scene photographs
of blood blotting the suburban rambler's hallway.

Calm and contrite, he resembles a parish priest,
not the tough Vietnam vet from whose temper
she once cowered. And it's almost Shakespearean
now, the way he wrings his hands, as if enough
conviction could somehow wash them clean.

Oniomania

Not so much the desire
for owning things
as the inability to choose
between hunter or emerald
green, to buy
just roses, when there are birds
of paradise, dahlias,
delphinium, and baby's breath.
At center an emptiness
large as a half-off sale table.
What could be so wrong
with a little indulgence?
To wander the aisles of fresh
new good things knowing
any of them could be hers?
With a closet full of shoes
unworn back home,
she's looking for love
but it's not for sale —
so she grabs three of
the next best thing.

Scrabbling

Hush. Shush. No mumbling please.
I'm searching for a hook, a vowel
dump, a U for this orphaned Q.

I've looked at every two to make three, every four to make five —
hoping for the pianissimo of PI, PIA, PIAN, PIANO.

I've considered every word from AA
to ZYZZYVAS, from AI to UNAU (both sloths)
but still can't find a good play from this mess.

Gadzooks! She just drew SATIRE and a blank.
Shall I count the ways I could have played that?

I know a REQUIN's a shark. A REBOZO's a scarf.
I watch her play STRENGTH for a triple-
triple, use my FIFTH to produce SIXTHLY
from a dead draw of consonants.

As I suffer multiple racks of E's,
she gleefully plays AVOCADO, TOSTADA,
CODICIL — and with her next turn lays down
GUACAMOLES across all three.

Should I trade it all in? Fish
for a bingo? Concoct a plausible phony?

Oh, what I'd give to make her EX
into EXECRABLE, build ANTIQUARIAN
around her QUA, change her AHA
into TOMAHAWKED.

The Devil's Dictionary of Medical Terms

after Ambrose Bierce, 1842–?1914

Allergies: Large lies. Eager ills.

Antibiotics: Is it botanic?

Antidepressant: President Satan.

Appendicitis: Septic 'n' I paid.

C-section: Nice cost.

Chronic Fatigue Syndrome: Oh, my secure grand fiction!

Depression: Snide poser. Person dies.

Dementia: I'd eat men. Detain me.

Dermatitis: Am dirtiest.

Diabetes Mellitus: Diet abuses met ill.

Erectile Dysfunction: Lucifer's indecent toy.

Flatulence: Clean flute.

Gastroenteritis: Rattiest regions.

Gall Stones: Lost angels.

Heart Attacks: That's a racket.

Hepatitis: I spit hate.

Hypertension: Shy inner poet.

Lower Back Pain: Incapable work.

Manic Depressive: Impressive dance.

Migraine: I'm in rage.

Neurotic: Unerotic.

Night Sweats: Things waste.

Nocturnal Enuresis: Encounters urinals. In unclean trousers.

Prostate Cancer: Crap! Not as erect. Procreates? Can't.

Renal Failure: Funereal lair.

Surgery: Guys err.

Tension Headache: Death's inane echo.

Uterine Prolapse: Plenteous repair.

Vasectomy: My octaves!

Whiplash Injury: Shh! I win jury, pal.

X-ray Department: Darn pretty exam.
Yeast Vaginitis: It's a nasty I give.
Zoonotic Diseases: Societies and zoos.

Genesis
Gin Sees

In the beginning, God created the heavens and the earth.
In the benign gin, God the servant threatened headache.

Now the earth was formless and empty, darkness was over the surface
        of the deep, and the Spirit of God was hovering over the waters.
Now the self-weary mad sportsman draws snakes over the perfect
        deaf house, and the frigid stoop was sovereign over the wrath.

And God said, Let there be light, and there was light.
And God said, The tiger! The bell! Light-hearted swan!

God saw that the light was good, and He separated the light from the
        darkness.
God, aghast, saw hot wild ghetto, and He spared the deathless king
        from threat.

God called the light day, and the darkness he called night. And there
        was evening, and there was morning, the first day.
God gladly ate the child, and the scathing hells darkened. And hate
        wins revenge, and hot warm sneering, the day's rift.

Reconsidering the Seven

Deadly Sins? Please — let's replace Pride
with Modesty, especially when it's false.

And thank goodness for Lust, without it
I wouldn't be here. Would you?

Envy, Greed — why not? If they lead us
to better ourselves, to Ambition.

And Gluttony, like a healthy belch, is a guest's
best response to being served a good meal.

I'll take Sloth over those busybodies
who can't sit still, watch a sunset

without yammering, or snapping a picture.
Now *that* makes me Wrathful.

Holy Shit

It used to be more private — just the
immediate family gathered after mass,
the baptismal font at the rear
of the church tiny as a bird bath.
The priest would ladle a few teaspoons'
tepid holy water on the bundled baby's
forehead, make a crack about the halo
being too tight as the new soul wailed.
We'd go home to pancakes and eggs.

These days it's a big Holy-wood production —
midmass, the giant altar rolls back to reveal
a Jacuzzi tub surrounded by potted palms.
The priest hikes up his chasuble, steps
barefoot out of his black leather loafers
and wades in like a newfangled John as
organ music swells and the baby-bearing families
line up like jumbo jets ready for takeoff.

But when the godparents handed my niece's newborn
naked to their parish priest, and he dunked her
into the Jacuzzi's bath-warm holy water,
her little one grew so calm and blissful she
pooped — not a smelly three-days' worth, explosive
diaper load, but enough to notice. As the godparents
scooped the turds with a handkerchief,
the savvy priest pretended he hadn't seen,
swept through the fouled water with his palm
before the next baby in line was submerged.

After mass, my niece sat speechless,
red-faced, not knowing what to say —
or whether — as church ladies, friends, and
family members presented one by one to

the tub where the babies had been
baptized. As they knelt and bowed
and dipped their fingers in,
and blessed themselves.

Lost in Translation

Before devising, your chicken you do not have to count.
As for the penny which is rescued it is the penny which is obtained.
The girl and the spice has become entirely from the splendid sugar.
The boy has consisted of the tail of the slug and the snail and the puppy.
As for the place of the woman there is a house.
One basket your egg everything does not have to be made.
The idiot hurries being about you fear because the angel steps on.
Your cake cannot do possessing and is eaten thing.
There is no wastefulness, unless so is, we want.
The safe which is better than regrettable.
Living, you have lived, permit.

Fugue

this is just to say I saw the icebox and wheels
rumbling through the figure 5
I saw the white chickens
in the dark city glazed with rain
I saw the figure 5 in the white chickens
the plums that were in gold on a red wheel barrow
the plums that you were probably
saving among the rain water
I have eaten the dark city so sweet
the plums that were so sweet
this is just to say I have eaten the figure 5
in the plums that so much depends
that were in gold on a red firetruck

Think or Swim

It's a short trip between artist and autist.
A sneak's a snake in disguise.
Poetry without the why is just trope.
I don't know whether we don't know what
we don't know, or merely need reminding.
I want to put the iron back in irony
— or at least the *noir*. To know how terror
leads to error, and defies to deifies.
I can't decide whether I'm not
thinking clearly or clearly not thinking.
Sometimes you just have to dive in
feetfirst. Like his mother said: Take the I
out of pitiful — you get uplift.

Webster's New Words: 2003

This dot-commer turned barista
with a killer app, whose portfolio
ain't worth bubkes, whose bubble burst
with nary a dead-cat bounce; this
headhunter with golden handcuffs
whose Frankenfood is giving me agita;
this botoxed exfoliant cack-handed agony aunt
selling heart-healthy fen-phen (better def
than phat); this mosh-pit goth headbanger
in a gimme cap; this NIMBY tweener with a brewski
has bogarted my junk DNA identity —
and now I'm on the fast track to a dog's
breakfast. I guess it's better than a McJob.

Anagrammer II

I'm interested in the space between
detonation and denotation.

I'm curious how things move
from ignored to eroding,
and from eroding to redoing.

How it is we make danger
into garden and
words into worlds.

So much depends
upon a letter lost or gained.
How we choose to parse
a phrase, spare
or spear a thought.

I want to know
how mystery leads to mastery
and poverty to poetry.

How we find the *g*
that makes enraged engaged.

How we know
whether to flee
or feel.

Alchemy

Late winter night cold as stone —
the wisteria unwinds its cord, budding store
-house of whispers. Corm shapes of crocus stare
and whimper under a dorm of stars.
Their drowsy simper a form that sears
into a simmer the worm hears.
Summer coming to swarm the heart.

Turning Straw into Gold

1

straw   strap   strip   grip   grill   gill   gild   gold

2

straw

       stalk

              haunt

                     field

                            realm

                                    wealth

                                            gold

3

Surely easier in the saying
than the doing. You go
rolling down the hill
and for what? To find
whom?

4

Time's up. Retreat now into neutral gray
season, to reappear again when
ice needles thaw on
green of longer days.

5

Why straw?
Who is this evil dwarf?
When will I learn his name?
How can such difficulty teach?
What does it mean to be locked in a room,
bid by the king to spin gold?

6

The winter fields are bare.
Across the sky a flash of amber,
a few piped notes.
The word for this time is:
Take up your bundle
and head for home.

Body Talk

While the ear may hear what
the head heard, lips can slip or lisp.

Wrists will twist or twirl while
the hand writes the wriest writs —
lamps-lit palms opening to psalms.

But when the spine is supine
and the penis ripens, the mind
neither snipes nor opines.

Inside the head's a shade
minding its own brainy binary ways.
Its nervy image of a mouth

will hum to itself. With no I inside,
merely a barn housing bran.

*

Do you hear how the scalp claps?
How the heart contains the earth, yet
is also a hater? How saliva
is lava, while testicles sit elect
for their slice test.

Do knees need to kneel?
Do toes toe or tow the line?
Are hands made to handle
our fingers' fringes?

The veins' vines climb. It takes guts
to tug at the pancreas' pear cans,
the pineal's spaniel, the liver's
silver sliver.

Arms and legs almost
a gnarled mess, foot & ankle
asleep in their fetal nook,
the shoulder a holder of us.

*

I'm tangles, my ligaments are out of alignment!
Be gentle with my genitals, they're not
made of gelatin. They give me a tingle
when I tango, with its angle all aglisten.

Look — his eyelids hid lies, yes. The prostate
a protest, a tart pose, 'cos umbilicus makes
a bilious music.

Keep your elbow below your bowel.
Our bone marrow a maroon brew,
like a warm robe on.

Remember hips are the ship
of the pelvis's lives. A breast
can be a star. Ovaries make
a *via eros,* or so I rave. But it's
the uterus contains the true us.

Weekend Healing

I like my attitude at this altitude.
The pool is open, but nobody
is swimming. I want to be better,
not bitter. I'm looking
for my armchair shaman, my
couch physician. Why do
today what you can
put off until tomorrow?
After all, an aphorism
a day keeps the dogma away.

II. PRACTICING

Laying On of Hands

The patient was talking.
I was listening and I wasn't.

Something about an extra piece of bone
inside his head. One eye that won't track.

Something about something stuck in her throat, how her heart
in the night whispers *silly lady, silly lady* . . .

The patient was talking about her . . . about his . . .
The patient was talking and I was watching

a mouth move. Was noticing the eyes, the hands
and their color, just how the breathing.

The patient was talking and I was not
hearing a sound. But I was listening and

I was there. I was standing beside and I was
listening with my hands.

Scald

Her toddler's pulled a pot
of boiling noodles onto himself.

Now she's screaming in the ER
as his chest and belly bubble,
his peeling genitals and thighs
turn scarlet — her Spanish a litany
of coyote howls and moans.

She does not understand,
watching her baby's skin slough,
why we need her to leave him
now, go with the social worker,
let us do our task.

The IV pierces the boy's forearm.
The oxygen mask covers his face.
His beautiful face.

I think to myself: At least
it spared
his face.

Beauty Mark

The grandmother wants me to excise
a little freckle like a teardrop
just below her granddaughter's left eye.
Too much sadness, she says, suggesting
through the interpreter that if I do not
she will cut it out herself —
It's our culture belief.

I tell her: In *my* culture
we call this a beauty mark —
to remove it, purely cosmetic,
uncalled for with a child.

But the grandmother persists, herself
a survivor of Pol Pot's camps.
Several visits we argue back and forth. My
usual compasses: First Do No Harm,
Autonomy Trumps Beneficence,
Lose the Battle of Initiative
all fail me. I begin to weaken.

What is my duty to protect a child?
And what exactly am I
protecting her from? (Surely, finger-pricks
and immunizations carry as much risk
as a simple mole removal.)

I agree to do a shave-excision,
hoping to leave the tiniest scar.
Weeks later, the grandmother shows me
her granddaughter's unblemished cheek, claps her palms
together to thank me. Years later, I still wonder
if what we did was right.

Nursemaid's Elbow

Named not for the mother, frazzled and rushed,
nor for the toddler who knows just when to flop.

Not for the swinging up from her tantrum,
nor for how swiftly it happens, the soft

chicken-wing pop. Not for the child
silent in ER, unable to lift

her left arm, nor for the X-ray showing
her radius slipped from its usual spot.

Not for the doctor cupping her elbow,
turning her palm back and up. Not for his thumb

finessing the ligament, nor for how
soon she's playing again with her dolls. But

for this: stern servant, hired helpstress, easy
scapegoat — the one who was not even there.

Inattentive

Forgets to do her chores, prefers to play
alone, loves to read but cannot finish
a book, traces rows of curlicues
on her Pee-Chee during class, knows
all the answers but is too petrified
to speak, and when spoken to at home
gazes glassily into space saying, *Yes,
Mother,* but hasn't grasped a word.

One day, sent to the garden to cut
a sprig of rosemary for potatoes,
she was half an hour later found
perched on grass-stained knees, scissors
lost, errand unremembered, her lips
kissing dandelion pom-poms into air.
Is she normal? The mother wants to know.
Uninclined to diagnose, to label,

I listen as her child recounts
a typical day at school, her favorite story —
She's obviously smart enough
to read the exam room's every pamphlet.
Is she *gifted?* Just a *fidget?* Who's to say
what's weed, what's wildflower? She
seems to me more dreamy than distracted:
lost thinking her long, long thoughts.

What the Skin Cutter Feels

Nothing but numb, the world's
pitch and yaw groaning inside her,
tense as an edge, a strange
smell like singed wires
everywhere, a deafening
silence, her mind a hive.

She reaches for a towel,
caresses the razor
between fingertips, imagines
the blade gliding over her thigh,
the hairless expanse of a wrist.

How she wishes this
inside wound were
outside — where
she could feel it,
watch it heal.

An urge that won't go away
until she lets it out —
a trickle of blood marking
her stunned flesh, as if to say: This
is where the world ends.

Practicing

1. Christmas Week

We come like the Magi paying homage,
before this eighty-year-old
woman with no family of her own.

Cedar swags and twinkling lights frame
the white hospital bed where she reclines,
one palm resting upon her swollen belly.

Over three days I've tapped her abdomen
for 14 liters, and still the fluid
keeps accumulating.

The sonographer wonders
if he sees a stellate mass blocking the blue
sky of her vena cava — but it isn't

there. We search for cirrhosis, ovarian
cancer, fungus, TB — nothing pans out.
She jokes that we should give her a spout

so she can drain herself
each morning, relieve her tummy's
distending ache. GYN, GI, ID,

Renal, Cards, Heme-Onc —
all the Wise Men drop by to visit, but
cannot solve, nor resolve,

her dissolving. *Where is all the water*
coming from? one of the nurses asks.
We can't explain it, I say. *It's*

a mystery. And it's true,
everyone who sees her comes away
mystified.

2. Restraint

He shrieks, kicks, wraps both arms
across his chest, shakes his head a defiant *No.*
We coax and cajole, offer stickers and stars, but he's
five, will not let us touch whatever plugs his nose.

I glance at the nasal speculum,
the vial of decongestant, useless
upon the standing tray, let him calm himself
with mother while the nurse and I huddle.

Soon we're pinning him down
on the exam table, the nurse clutching elbows
up about his ears as I lean upon thrashing legs,
cast a fiber-optic beam upon his face.

He's trapped in the light, the nurse steadies his head,
as I edge toward his nose with the toothed forceps.
His howling falls silent, and I notice his eyes, glaring at me,
enraged and defiant. He snorts and I glimpse

the thing we are looking for — I probe,
nudge, grasp the pink, firm . . . *pencil eraser?*
and pull it out, glistening with snot.
In a moment he's back in mother's arms, tears

brushed away, smiling for his treat. Whether I'm forgiven
or forgotten, it's as if none of this has happened —
I tousle his hair, he tears the plastic wrapper
And, smiling, licks his sticker.

3. Aspiration

Breast swabbed with iodine, her nipple
erect as the lidocaine makes its numbing
wheal, she reclines with her right elbow
folded behind her head, regards the poster
of Italy pinned to the ceiling, begins
to tell me of the summer she hiked
the Cinque Terre. But when the needle
of my aspirator hits something firm
and stops, our offhand chatter halts.
She is pale as a cloud. *Take a deep breath —
then exhale slowly,* I say, holding the mass
firmly between thumb and forefinger,
slowly twirling the needle's hub. *What is it?*
she asks. Before I can answer, a sudden gush
fills the syringe with straw-colored fluid
and the lump is gone quick as a sigh
leaving a room. We'll wait for the path lab's
verdict, the mammogram, but for now
this is good news. I tell her to cut back
on caffeine and chocolate, eat less fat,
but she's already gone, lifting her
two-year-old into living arms.

4. Beneficence

The home health nurse tells me the house
is a disaster — newspapers stacked, not a clean dish,
rodent shit in the corners and mold on the walls,
three hungry dogs, five cats, their hair
everywhere: in the bedding, in the kitchen,
glued to the open sores on his swollen legs.
Half a dozen insulin syringes litter the hall floor,
pills lie scattered out of bottles on tables
in the living room — who knows which
ones he is and is not taking. The filthy
bathroom has no running water, its belching
sink stoppered with a mayonnaise lid. And now
he refuses to let anyone come in and help,
afraid it'll only be the beginning of more
losses — like the serial amputations,
first one big toe, then the other, then
both feet even when he said no.
No, he's not letting anyone else in.
Not again.

5. Nothing's Broken

She's drunk, covered with bruises,
won't say one way or another
who did this to her or why, refuses
to let me call the police,

a social worker, or counselor.
Through swollen lips she mumbles
something about a dealer,
her ex-husband, how

all she really wants
is X-rays, something for the pain,
and not to be
asked so many questions.

She returns from radiology,
blue hospital gown slipping from her
bare right shoulder, an ice pack
covering her left eye. Dressed in my white coat

and clipboard, I tell her, *The good news —*
nothing's broken, but it neither comforts nor consoles.
She calls her sister for a ride home, but disappears
out the back door before she arrives.

6. Exit Wound

Who makes a coffee table out of glass?
he asks, holding a dish towel
wrapped around his bloodied hand.

We chat about nothing
as I irrigate the tidy lacerations, test
his tendons, suture the skin shut.

I jot a picture of the gashes
next to my note, ask him
to return in a week for

me to remove his stitches.
Next day a detective arrives
to see what I have written.

The man's wife is dead —
strangled as she crashed through
the living room's glass table.

The wounds on her
husband's hands
the only evidence.

7. Precip

Head wrapped in traditional Muslim veil,
soaked skirt gathered about her hips,
she squats on her kitchen's yellow linoleum floor,
mud-colored blood and amnion
pooling as she cradles a shivering

newborn barely two minutes old — his eyes
wide open, blue fingers resting upon a pink
and wrinkled brow, as if he's considering
what best to say
to this stranger's hovering face.

I time the heart rate, count
a dozen whimpering but healthy breaths.
One of the firemen clamps the cord
as I cut through it with bandage scissors,
pass the baby to a neighbor's warm bath towel.

Kneeling between her legs, I feel something warm
soak my trouser knee, trace the winding
umbilical cord up to her swollen labia, where
a rivulet of fresh blood paints a jagged stream.
I tug gently and the placenta plops out —

but the bright red continues to gush.
One of the firemen cusses as he flubs another IV.
The color drains from the woman's face.
Acting on instinct and survival, she arches her back
as I push my gloved fist into her vagina,

cup her uterus from above with my palm,
massaging the spongy tissue until it draws tight.
Her uterine torrent slows to a trickle.
The mother opens her eyes and smiles —
and then we hear the baby cry.

Case History: Persephone

The visiting surgery resident
inserts the icy speculum
while the mother stands nearby
clutching her only daughter's pale hand.
Outside the window — a barren
January day. The long fields lie empty,
their edges stitched with bare trees.

The resident repeats the history:
less clarification than compulsive ritual.
No. There had been nothing unusual.
The girls had watched a video, shared a
bowl of buttered popcorn, played a game
of Truth or Dare.

He asks again about boys
and the girl blushes dark as a fresh bruise.
Then she remembers the three
pomegranate seeds she swallowed whole.
A spasm doubles her as she wretches
and heaves — her mother in a fury —
Hurry, doctor. She's burning up!

The ultrasound's sonar beam
reveals the dark haze buried
near the cavern of her cecum — yet
it is still not proof enough. The mother
will not relent until up to our wrists in blood
we deliver it to her
in a formalin jar — the offending
appendix, red and swollen as a worm.

Damn Fag

I've heard his story before. How a car
accident broke his spine
in three places, but the X-rays
and MRI don't show it.

How he's tried rehab, counseling, physical therapy.
How all he wants now is some OxyContin
and I'm not giving it. *Then we're*
through here, he says, and I close his file.

Damn fag, he mutters
as he exits the exam room.
The words sting. Even in my white coat,
shielded by my stethoscope and tie.

Two words and I am in high school again,
backed against a locker,
coat collar clenched.

I'm in residency and the attending
surgeon is holding court over the open abdominal wound
of a young man with AIDS,

saying — for my benefit: *When cattle*
get an infection like this
we put them all *to sleep.*

Damn fag. How did he
know? Was it written
across my face?

Even after all these years.
Why am I ashamed?

The Push

Unassisted in ER 4, curtain pulled,
I'm suturing the head lac of another drunk
who's cussing at me and the world,
the reek of his breath penetrating
even the fenestrated drape, my mask.
I ask him nicely to please hold still sir
so I can clean the wound, inject the lidocaine,
please hold still sir, don't touch that it's sterile,
even through the four-point restraints
he's thrashing, *damn* I have to reglove
now, *hold still,* please keep your head
on the pillow sir, doesn't he understand
I'm trying to help? It's late, I'm
tired, and there's three more to see
after him, *damn it, hold still!*
And then that moment — where I grasp
his shoulders perhaps a little too firmly,
rip the drape from his face so he can
see me: *I'm not going to say this
one more time. Do you understand?*
And even through his drunken stupor
he understands. I know he understands.
The ugly part of this relationship.
This potential to do harm.
And he laughs, almost mocking.
And lets me continue.

What's Written on the Body

He will not light long enough
for the interpreter to gather
the tatters of his speech.
But the longer we listen
the calmer he becomes.
He shows me the place where his daughter
has rubbed with a coin, violaceous streaks
raising a skeletal pattern on his chest.
He thinks he's been hit by the wind.
He's worried it will become pneumonia.
In Cambodia, he'd be given
a special tea, a prescriptive sacrifice,
the right chants to say. But I
know nothing of Chi, of Karma,
and ask him to lift the back of his shirt,
so I may listen to his breathing.
Holding the stethoscope's bell I'm stunned
by the whirl of icons and script
tattooed across his back, their teal green color
the outline of a map which looks
like Cambodia, perhaps his village, a lake,
then a scroll of letters in a watery signature.
I ask the interpreter what it means.
It's a spell, asking his ancestors
to protect him from evil spirits —
she is tracing the lines with her fingers —
and those who meet him for kindness.
The old man waves his arms and a staccato
of diphthongs and nasals fills the room.
He believes these words will lead his spirit
back to Cambodia after he dies.
I see, I say, and rest my hand on his shoulder.
He takes full deep breaths and I listen,

touching down with the stethoscope
from his back to his front. He watches me
with anticipation — as if awaiting a verdict.
His lungs are clear. *You'll be fine,*
I tell him. *It's not your time to die.*
His shoulders relax and he folds his hands
above his head as if in blessing.
Ar-kon, he says. *All better now.*

Radiation (the Sun Room)

Twenty small tumors scattered in his brain,
one for each year he continued to smoke

after the doctors advised him to quit.
Now his head's cradled in a mesh helmet

bolted to the oncologist's table.
When the 200-pound lead door slams shut

and he is alone with the gray monster,
its lone eye focused on his tattooed scalp,

he tells me he sees a white beach, waves crashing,
a breeze parting his imaginary hair.

Tremor

Because she took an extra scoop of rice
the soldiers made her watch
while one of them held a machete,
swung it into her uncle's neck.
Don't close your eyes or we'll shoot you!
they said. She remembers how his face
grimaced, his eyes still blinking
as his head tumbled toward her.
How his legs kicked as if his body
were still trying to run away.
How can the body move without
the head? she asks, referring to her left arm —
the way it rocks back and forth
when she rests it on her lap. How
it stops when she reaches
for her teacup, her chopsticks.
I cup her elbow in my palm, feel
the ratcheting as I flex her forearm
forward and back; notice
how her eyes seem to gaze
at a faraway place, her face
unyielding as a stone Buddha.
I do not know how to ease or erase
what war has written in her memory,
but her tremor should lessen
with the right medicine. And that hope
seems to bring her a moment's peace.

Tic Douloureux

For weeks, months, he feels nothing.
Then a slight breeze brushes his face,
he absentmindedly strokes his mustache
or a grandchild kisses his cheek,
and the ice pick stabs just below his left eye,
making him wince and water, spasming
his face into lopsided grimace.

No one can tell him why it pokes
him, how long it will last, or who gave it
such a glamorous name. But we all agree it's excruciating.
Worse than birth pains, or a kidney stone.
This sudden electric shock like
a drill bit spinning against his zygoma.
This burnt matchstick held to his eyelid.

The medicines we try only make him sleepy.
And the nerve surgery, rhyzolysis,
could paralyze half his face.

Just when he thinks he can't take it anymore — it vanishes.
For weeks, months, he feels nothing.
Sometimes a year passes and he almost forgets.

Then, reading a book one evening,
or gazing at some family photos, he turns to watch
a hummingbird at the feeder, an eyelash
falls and grazes his cheek —
a little tickle, that sends him.

Y

1

Much-maligned garbage
heap, barren wasteland of repeating
beads of DNA. Mere
placeholder.

A fragile thing, easily broken.
Unable to pair like the other chromosomes,
repair its dinged-up nucleotides,
tagging along with its mismatched X.

Boy's first gift from his father·
78 genes encoding the production
of sperm, and not much else.

2

When two Xs meet
in metaphase, they touch everywhere,
depend upon each other, share
everything, like old girlfriends
exchanging recipes or gossip.

But when X and Y pair
it's uneven, unbalanced:
He's a cartoon muscleman, all
shoulders & arms and a skinny little body.
Her four limbs too much for him.

They only touch at one end. He has
so little to offer her. So little that
many believe he may one day become
obsolete. Superfluous
as a husband holding a purse
outside the women's restroom door.

3

But now we learn there may be more
to Y than meets the eye.
His few genes a kind of palimpsest
parsing forward, backward, upside down.

Sequences of nucleotides origami-ed
into new readings, skipped sections folded back
to generate new texts, neighboring sections
pairing up, rebuilding themselves —
the seemingly nonsensical

perhaps a kind of source code, an entire world
built from palindromes and puzzles.

Why a man says: *I can
take care of myself.*

Why he's the ultimate multitasker:
watching the ball game and planning a porch redo,
calling his mother on the cell and
eating a ham sandwich — all while seeming
to be doing nothing at all.

Attending Rounds

She woke in the night with an elephant
on her chest took three nitroglycerin
dialed 911 got four of morphine
in the field then rolled into the ER
V-fib arrest ongoing CPR
was shocked three times at death's gummed door before
her heart's jingle-jangle rhythm returned.

Now upright in her bedside chair eating
a blueberry pancake sipping orange juice
all she remembers of the night's wild ride
is dreaming a giant bee was stinging
her left shoulder — then waking bolt up
in a strange bed an even stranger room
to ask: *Honey, have you seen my purse?*

Dream of the Cancer Cure

Imagine: instead of fighting the tumor
with knives, radiation, chemicals,
we feed it — like summer picnickers who,
tired of swatting the buzzing swarm,
lay out a separate plate of meat
and cheeses for the bees.

While the tumor calmly swells
onto its bedside petri dish of food, nourished
by every plasma and mineral it needs,
you lie in bed — read *People,* knit a scarf,
chat with your aunt Ezgi on the phone.

Until one day the cancer is no longer *in* you
at all — but a pulsing mass grown separate
on its tray, that the surgeon will cut free,
severing veins and arteries that once
bound it to you like a baby. Deliver you of it —
carry it howling and dripping away.

III. BUDDLEIA

Butterfly Bush

I used to love the buddleia,
its long purple trumpets in summer
buzzing with hummingbirds and butterflies,

until someone told me it was *common,*
invasive, a weed —

its withered flower cones
spilling armies of seedlings
to colonize the neighborhood.

Then I was embarrassed to have loved it.

I began to see its offspring sprouting
everywhere, hated how they rooted
between loose bricks, flourished
from cracks in the sidewalk.

So I cut mine back to nothing,
buried the broken stump —

only to find it returned
the next spring, multiplied.

And though I hated it
then, a part of me wanted it
to live. So I resolved to remove

the spent flowers, trim the branches.
Each autumn its size diminished,
and each spring an open

relaxed shape returning.
Its abundance held in check.

And now I love the buddleia
again as before,
but by second nature —
as one who returns to the garden
after the fall.

Abandoned Lot

Unbuildable, steep, wooden stairway collapsing
along its north side, trees crawling with ivy.
Haunt of high-schoolers smoking pot,
their empty beer bottles discarded
among sprung mattresses, the occasional
used condom found littering the path.
A roll of chain-link rusts in one corner
where an avocado refrigerator
lies dumped on its back,
door flung open like a grave.

Next to our tended yards and homes,
our utterly intentional lives, this cast-off
wayward place, unplanned, junk-strewn,
seems a kind of refuge. Nature taking over,
filling in the empty spaces:
Scotch broom, grasses, wild nettle thicket.
Home to the blue jay, the woodpecker.
In hottest summer a place to stop,
rest in the ash's rampant shade,
savor the season's first ripe blackberry

The Scholar's Garden

We wander past water-worn
limestone, gnarled pine. Delicate
bamboo rustles over a jade-colored pool,
where goldfish swim amid
the cherry's dipping branches.

We must return to the train
by three, yet I cannot bring myself
even to look at my watch.

Sitting on the cedar bench, I study
spiral forms in gravel, imagine
we are no longer tourists, but ancient
Chinese philosophers at ease
in a walled garden, stroking
the characters of poems onto scrolls,
suspended here as if in amber.

Before us the plum's weathered stump.
New shoots swaying with blossoms.

The Garden Buddha

Gift of a friend, the stone Buddha sits zazen,
prayer beads clutched in his chubby fingers.
Through snow, icy rain, the riot of spring flowers,
he gazes forward to the city in the distance — always

the same bountiful smile upon his portly face.
Why don't I share his one-minded happiness?
The pear blossom, the crimson-petaled magnolia,
filling me instead with a mixture of nostalgia

and yearning. He's laughing at me, isn't he?
The seasons wheeling despite my photographs
and notes, my desire to make them pause.
Is that the lesson? That stasis, this holding on,

is not life? Now I'm smiling, too — the late cherry,
its soft pink blossoms already beginning to scatter;
the trillium, its three-petaled white flowers
exquisitely tinged with purple as they fall.

Lettuce Weather

We scratch a tiny furrow with a stick,
pinch in our favorite mesclun mix,
drizzle in clear water from a hose, then
lightly pat the soil with bare palms.
Such springy ritual, showing faith in
a world returning to life. Forsythia
branches cast yellow petals. Two jays
scrummage in the white lilac for twigs.
Our elderly neighbor feels spry enough
to climb a ladder and wash her windows
(we rush over to help!) while her grandson
wheels out his motorbike for a ride. Yes —
that vacant lot up the street's for sale again.

Aesop's Dog

What is a bridge but a way to cross
over? And what is a river but a thing to be
crossed amid shimmers? Why did I look?
And after looking, why want? I carried
the most perfect bone in my jaws.
The meat glistened. I gnawed its shaft,
tasted its dark marrow, dreamed myself
home — with water dish and blanket, feasting
in peace and solitude. What made me look
away? And after looking, why want
what the other had? The bridge was so near,
the water was so bright. One bone or two?
When I heard the splash, I knew.

Dante Reconsiders *Paradise*

Of course, my task was formidable,
making eternal bliss seem interesting.
Without Virgil I was reduced to mere apology.
Yet who except the already damned
would find an eternity of grace
among pale angels engaging?
Especially when he could be jousting in Hell,
limbs endlessly hacked and then healed;
or circling Purgatory's seven terraces
meting out a slow but sure century
of forgiveness. Perhaps even then I knew
how humans need to suffer, will choose
wandering a dark labyrinth over endless
contemplation of a rose.

The Judas Tree

Tell me about the sin of pride
and I'll tell you
about the lie of forgiveness.

Ai, "Two Brothers"

Would it be enough to say
I was afraid? That I stood accused,
wrists bound, eyes blackened?
That centurions led me to a high balcony,
showed me the throng
swarming for Passover, and you
among them, riding a donkey?

You love him? they jeered,
and spit in my face. *Then*
kiss him, they hissed,
and knocked me to the floor.

Rose welts streaked the dawn
as I dangled. And later, red flowers
pierced my thorned limbs
in your honor.

To hell with dreams of silver,
with your magical fall that lifts us
from the muck. Without a lover
there is no beloved.

The Young Priest

Your years at Immaculata could never
have prepared you for this
small a parish, so far from heaven.

What agony to stand before them,
robed in purple, holding the tin chalice
amid its hosanna of flies.

> *Lamb of God, who takes away*
> *the sins of the world, have mercy on us.*
>
> *Lamb of God, who takes away the sins . . .*
>
> *Lamb of God, who takes . . .*
> *grant us peace.*

The village boy spreads open the book
and you touch it with your lips,
trying to forget where your mouth
has been, what forbidden
creases it has tasted.

(Remember: You are only a man,)

This is my body.

(it was only a moment)

This is my blood.

(of bliss.)

You answer each tongue
with a pallid host.

Mount Baker in August

White peaks float
upon a layer of cloud,
like our small idea of heaven.

Gazing at the mountain
makes my mind feel empty
as the lake I wouldn't have seen
had I driven the other way.

Two errors in perceiving
the world this way:
First, seeing only a mirror
of the self. Then, not seeing
the self as part of the world.

It opens a cleft inside.
And something shadowed begins.

The way a scorpion will hide
in a conch's dark hollow.
Death disguised as beauty.

The Corpse Flower

Amorphophallus titanum

Like the carrion beetles needed to fertilize it,
we've traveled for miles not merely to see
but to smell this colossally fetid flower
the Sumatrans named Devil's Tongue.
The marooned-tinged spathe has unwrapped,
dropped its skirt around the five-foot-long spadix
with its erection of small blooms. Opened, the tomb
tempts us. Like children wanting a scare at Halloween,
or lovers at a horror flick, we hold our breath.
The bravest unplug their noses and take a whiff.
Rotten fish composted with toe cheese and bean farts.
Nature's smelliest plant oils and various sulfury
pitches. Peonies, honeysuckle, and jasmine
grace the air with pleasant scents. And for this
we love them. The corpse flower knows
we come from what has decomposed —
and like gawkers drawn to a car crash
can't keep ourselves away.

The Cruciverbalist

for Carol Folger 1956–2001

Sunday afternoon, *New York Times*
quarter-folded, a calico cat purring
on her lap, she sips a third cup of tea,
nibbles her pencil eraser, puzzled
by the way *felon* makes "some lips"
pulsed not *pursed,* wondering
if *juror* is what's meant
by "his verdict is read."

Say "bay" is *leaf,* then "spry" could be *frisky.*
But if "spry" is *lively* then "bay"
must be *howl.* And thinking "Sappho" *Aeolian*
rather than *aeonian,* puts an *L* in *bent,*
making "off-kilter" *belt.*

Such serious pleasure in the tangle
of clues and meanings,
this knitting together of letters like a scarf.
She loves how words work at cross-purposes,
how "buckle" can mean *fasten* or *fall in,*
"livid" both *pale* and *blue.*

How "mad about" is *love* or *hate,* depending
upon "refrain" meaning *stop*
or song. How through *hazard,*
loss, pain, and *evil* —
hope appears.

Night-blooming Cereus

for Carol

That summer you were home dying of breast cancer
the daily news shrieked of lightning-sparked
wildfires, hundred-year floods, and a
flurry of shark attacks in Florida —
a boy no older than your son, his arm
torn off one night as he played in the ocean.

And you with your arm swollen
and dead to you —
listening to it all on the radio,
sipping ice water through a straw,
the chemo making you puke,
propped among pillows in the guest room,
a part of you knowing we are all guests here.

One morning a woman on the freeway
bridge just blocks from your home
straddled the railing in the middle of rush hour
inciting a mile-long traffic jam —
irate motorists late for their jobs,
a heckling busload of commuters
goading her to jump.

How can people be so heartless? you asked.

Though you'd doctored others for years
you were uneasy speaking of your own death.
But later, through the fog of chemo and morphine,
you called one evening —
the cereus in your kitchen
was growing this most amazing flower,
the magnificent white bud slowly opening

before your eyes. And I should come quickly,
you didn't want me to miss it —
its dying fragrance soon to fill the house.

Breathing Lesson

The meditation instructor speaks of *ma,*
or emptiness — asks us to listen
to our breathing.
I think of the pleural space,
the vacuum our ribs and diaphragm
pull upon when we take in
breath, that pulls back when we exhale.
How we draw upon this emptiness,
and it draws upon us. How an anatomist
would call it a *potential space,* meaning
it does not exist — unless intruded upon.
How if our pleural lining is broken
we cannot breathe, until the surgeon
inserts a tube, restores the vacuum. How
it's said *nature abhors a vacuum,* yet
we cannot exist without one.
Without *ma.* Without this
emptiness within.

Hearts

The day nurse fishes in my mother's forearm
for a good IV site before letting the orderly
gurney her to surgery.

Surprised how black
her blood looks, we laugh about medieval humors —
how hers should be more *sanguine*.

The Valium pill is bitter, and difficult
for her to swallow, yet she wants
the sleep it brings.

She tells me again —
two months of vague pains in her left breast,
left arm. All her brothers with bypasses.

She remembers the day she set her teacup
back upon its saucer, went to wake
Father from his nap —
found him cold and pulseless.

The ugly chaos of medics in the living room
jolting him with electricity, their arms
plunging his lifeless chest.

As she trails off midmemory
I imagine the dye
shooting through her coronaries.

The arc of her life told
in a jagged flash of light, becoming
indelible as a crack in a china cup.

Burning the Nests

Atop an orchard ladder my father
stands half-hidden by the black cherry's
tangled branches, holding a gasoline-soaked
rag wrapped on the end of a broomstick.
He flicks open his silver lighter, tells us
to stand back as the torch ignites
and he thrusts the burning thing up
where the white nets of caterpillars
tent the upper branch tips. A terrible
crackling like singed hair
fills the early April evening
as we squeal, and the smoldering
bits of caterpillars fall to the ground.
Weeks later we will eat the spicy
meat of the cherries, not even thinking
of this carnage. Or if we do, only
as the kind of work that fathers
will do, for their children.

Crossing the Pear

for Arthur Pereira & Victor Perera

The summer I turned twelve, my father and I
discovered a half-eaten pear
sprouting from the compost.
We tied it to a fence, watered and watched
two branches appear, then four.

*

There are twenty-eight pages of Pereiras
in the Lisbon telephone book.

*

All summer and fall I watered, then one morning: nothing
but bent twigs shriveled.

*

In my parochial school history books
the Portuguese were beautiful men who dangled
gold hoops from earlobes and sailed
the seven seas. They told nothing
of the days of Inquisition, when for refusing pork,
or changing linen on Fridays, over 200 Pereiras
perished in Evora alone.

*

. . . the pear was forced into the mouth,
rectum, or vagina of the accused,
expanded by force of a screw
to the maximum aperture of its segments.

*

The venerable pear, my patronym.

Scattered across continents,
expulsed from garden to garden.
If flight is no more
than an admission of guilt,
what was our crime?

*

Youngest of five brothers, my father
stole rice from under the bayonets of Hong Kong's
Japanese invaders, attended Catholic mass with his widowed
     mother
every day but Saturday.

*

Twenty-eight pages of Pereiras:
the same as I would find in Rio,
São Paulo, Managua, Macau . . .

*

I bask in the shade of a spreading pear tree,
laden with new fruit. My father's name
is all that's left of him, a vague sweetness,
the taste of pear.

IV. NIGHT WALK

Ravenna at Dusk

Today when I looked in the mirror
I saw my father looking back.
I like walking alone at night.
One can be happy not only without love,
but despite it. It's best to fertilize roses
in March, plant gladioli bulbs in October.
I love the sound of thunder before rain.
Country-western dancing can be fun.
Oak floors with a Swedish finish last longest.
Espresso after six will keep you awake
past two. Antique floor lamps are cheap
at Capitol Hill garage sales in summer.
What can you do to give your life meaning?
It's useless to repair socks once the heels are out.
My married friends make babies because they can.
Bath towels stack best when folded in thirds.
I have always found the lives of mystics
and clerics more appealing. I still read
the funnies and sleep in late on Saturdays.
Life is not so much invented as composed.
In high school I loved my English teacher
and wrote my first poems for him.

Sweat Equity

Layers of green shag smothered oak hardwoods,
rolls of 1950s newspapers insulated
a basement stairway closet, aluminum-framed
windows with broken seals grew greenish algae.

But how else could we look back now upon
romantic weekends scraping layers of paint,
lovers quarreling over colors for siding, then
hanging new double-hungs.

Re-roofing, re-plumbing, re-wiring,
removing a false lowered ceiling:
not so much a revision
as a retelling,

adding to what had gone before,
working up the sweet sweat
that makes a relationship hum,
makes a place indelibly, undeniably yours.

It's how we come to inhabit where we are:
tearing down a wall, planting a tree,
brushing another coat of paint onto plaster,
lowering a hedge to reclaim a view.

Like when we wrote our names
onto the closet wall of the first apartment
we shared, before repaneling it with cedar —
we're still there, beneath the surface, built in.

Perfect Pitch

> "F . . . the oven is an F"
> *Samantha Foggle, age 3*

Oh, to hear the world with such clarity.
Such surety. To know the note
of your breakfast chat is B-flat minor.
That the '57 Chevy stalled outside the
garage is a D. To recognize the Apricot
kitchen paint for what it is: F-sharp.
To understand the way you feel for him is G,
definitely a G. And as you watch him
descend the scale of the front steps to his car
for work, the house quiets to an A.
The arpeggio of last night's Every
Good Boy Deserves Favor
still ringing in your ears.

Channeling Madge

for Dean

Months after his mother's funeral
odd turns of phrase
wend their ways into his mouth:
Howdy-do and *back at ya.*
This conversation's going into a hole.
He loses his keys,
his wallet. Becomes obsessed
with canning beans. Develops
a sudden affection for yarn,
stashing money in sock drawers.
You could buy that lot for a song
and sing it yourself. Entranced
by a branch of the flowering plum
he stands in the side yard
wearing an old kitchen apron,
both hands raised to the white sky
as if hanging wet linens
from a slackened clothesline.

After *The Pillow Book*

You call me to the bath, where
by evening light before bed I rub
the ointment into your maculate back.
I place my hand between the wings
of your scapulae, where you cannot
reach, cannot see — the arc of your life
revealed in its pattern of coffee-colored
spots — and hover there awhile,
remembering how we watched the lover
read the manuscript painted on the skin
of his beloved; how he pressed
the words to his chest and face   and cried out.
The arteries in my palm open, their warmth
rising between us as I massage you, neither
sexual nor umbilical,
this connection — you trusting
your back to me, and
me with no deceit.
Only salve, only unguent.
Only balm.

Missing *e*

Since you've been gone
I'm missing the *e*'s
that turn *rivers* into *reveries.*

Now *please* becomes *pleas,*
and my *emotions* are just *motions.*

I am trying to understand
the *lesson* in *one less.*

I'm missing the *e* that
turns *search* into *reaches,*

makes an *antique   quaint*
and *baudy* almost *beauty.*

Since you've been gone I'm missing
the *e* that makes *drama   a dream,*
and *climax   exclaim.*

I'm missing
the *e* that makes *breath*
breathe, and *last* not *least.*

Ganymede to Zeus

They say you're old enough
to be my father; that you hold me
here against my will.
But what could they know
of a shepherd boy's desires?
I'm more than happy to languish
forever in this temple, floating
among the marble and clouds, raptly
peeling grapes and sipping
from your mighty cup.
After all, you are a god, and I
your adored and adoring boy.
Remember the day you found
me? I was tending the spring flock.
Their lambing cries and the stench
rising from their damp fur
filled the morning air. *Oh, Daddy,*
I cried as your hot breath
grazed my neck and your eagle's
talons pierced my tender backside.
As the slumbering village disappeared
below, and I howled for sisters I'd never
see again, you whispered, *Ganymede will be Zeus'*
most perfect love. You pulled me closer
under wing, your warm belly firm
against my back, and I knew
you would fly me to heaven.

Devil's Bridge

Vultee Arch, Sedona, Arizona

Midday sun stuns the red road.
We leave our car shaded by cottonwoods,
follow a dry creek bed winding
through stunted piñon pine and juniper,
ghost in search of its source.

Wizened trunks of manzanita
twist silver from the hardpan,
the cool resilience of new branches
sure handholds as we climb
massive slabs of limestone stacked like plates,
the sweat spreading in our shirts,
each ledge opening a new vista
on the valley scribbled far below.

As you scramble up the steep slope,
picking our path through rubble and dust,
I think of Virgil leading Dante
upward through Hell's rifted rock
to the first mountain terrace of Purgatory,
the sun in declension, the souls of the dead
frightened by his body made of living flesh.

Our shadows stretch before us
when we spot it: a great spit of rock
eroded glacial millennia ago,
now a wing of stone arching the ravine.
We take turns capturing ourselves
arms raised, standing atop it.
Then cross as darkness gathers,
to whatever awaits us.

The Flowerless Branch

Each year a new spear
knifes up from the chips of bark,
rises, swells, sprouts delicate leaf pairs,
but still, no orchid flower.
We fertilize, water; don't fertilize,
don't water; move the pot
from dim hallway to bright living room —
and still: flowerless. Like us,
living without a child? Two men,
barren as a cuckoo and a mule.
Barren as a cuckoo and a mule
living without a child. Two men.
And still, flowerless, like us
from dim hallway to bright living room —
don't water; move the pot
we fertilize, water; don't fertilize.
But still no orchid flower
rises, swells, sprouts delicate leaf pairs,
knifes up from the chips of bark.
Each year a new spear.

Taken

I've doctored her through hip replacement,
colon cancer, stroke. She is the doting grandmother
I never had. Thinks of me as her virtuous, infallible
second son. So it's no surprise she notices immediately
at her monthly clinic visit the new gold band on my finger.
Do you have some news to tell me? Taken off guard,
I mumble something about anniversary gifts,
fifteen years, my partner. *Partner?* She turns
a worried, puzzled look toward her daughter.
Did he say partner? Surely, after all these years she knew
my preference. But now she seems disappointed. Almost
disapproving. Produces a picture from her billfold
of someone she and her daughter had hoped to introduce
to unmarried me. *Well,* she huffs, *you know
what they say, all the good ones are . . . taken.*
I wince, expecting to see a hazy glamour shot
of a favorite niece or neighbor, but to my surprise
and delight, the one they had imagined for me: a man.

Doppelgänger

1986/2006

Your picture that morning on every front page
next to the story that was written about you.
Then your face beaming from the window
of the car stopped by mine at our light.
How I smiled and you followed me home,
stayed after to watch *My Beautiful Laundrette.*

Stopped by the light on our front picture
window to watch your face next to mine.
Beaming then from the story about how you
and I stayed after at the laundrette that morning
your beautiful car smiled me home.
My every page that followed was written of you.

Twenty Years after His Passing, My Father Appears to Us in Chicago, at Bobby Chinn's Crab & Oyster House, in the Guise of Our Waiter, Ramon

He's much younger than I remembered — pearl black
hair grown long with a flip and some grease
to hold it in place — but I can tell it's him. He's dressed

more stylish than the rest: shoes shined, pants creased, natty tie
clipped to starched white shirt, gold cufflinks — and that pinky ring
he always loved to twist. When he vanishes to fetch our Lemon Drop

and Cosmo you ask me what's the matter and I whisper: *Ramon's
the reincarnation of my dad* . . . And though you've never
actually met him, except in family photographs,

you gasp that you were wondering the exact same thing!
Ramon returns promptly with our drinks, warns us, in my father's
odd accent, to avoid the *Sears Tower: too many touristas*. Recommends

instead the boat tour across the river, where we can view all the
doll buildings from the water. We order sea scallops and crab cakes.
He winks and whisks away our menus. But I can tell he's nervous,
            wants

everything to be perfect — his hands quiver as he divides our Caesar
at the table, a bead of sweat forming on his dark brow. The dinner is
            divine.
Magical. And to top it off, Ramon offers to buy dessert. But all I want
            is for my dad

to sit down and talk with us for a while. *Please,* he says, *it's on me.*
With that same disarming smile, button brown eyes, of my father
            selling fabric
and notions to shop ladies those years at Northgate Mall.

Only now I find it adorable. We order a chocolate raspberry torte,
a pair of cappuccinos. He knows to bring an extra fork. Tells us:
Be happy together. Folds two mints into our check.

October Journal

Pine boughs scattered on the lawn outside the window.

Leaves falling like particles of light,
as if composed purely of light.

I watch the windmill out back,
its tail-like rudder animated by the wind
                                    in search
of a position of least resistance, of quiet,
wandering as the living do, sent by the wind.

Purling fan blades shuttle like a loom,
purging the gully's rainwater up to feed
                                    the hillside's meandering stream,
until what moves them comes to a stop,
Fortune's wheel falling on zero, zippo, zilch.

                        *

First power outage of the year and I'm lost
shopping for pork roast and rosemary red potatoes
amid shelves draped with cobwebs and goblins,
plastic sacks of candy, the meat case garish in shadow
                                    like the back of an unlit closet.
An old man pushes an empty cart down the aisle,
gaunt and jaundiced,
his belly swollen like a starving child's,
                                his toothless mouth asking,

Which aisle is milk?

                        *

Spring amazed us with its soft parade of fragrance and color: but how brief
the azalea, the pink in the cherry.

Summer a long calm, a steady pouring forth.

And this year, easy September stretching long into October —
                                             unseasonable, warm.

The garden on a marathon: new sprigs of lobelia coming,
blades of tulip, hyacinth, and daffodil piercing the autumn soil.
The espaliered apple confused into setting fresh buds.
Ripe apples sharing the same branch as dead leaves, white blossoms,
new fruit forming.
                    An impossible diorama,
like the great still lifes of the old masters:
flower, fruit, and fowl from the entire year
                              captured together on one table.
Image of the infinite.
As if all time were present outside of time, a glorious hoax,
                                             a higher reality.

                                *

Can nature ever be wrong?
Autumn a gold tone across the sky, the trees burnished. An illuminated
     manuscript.

The warm days drawing the sap into the leaves,
                              the sumac, sugar maples, flaming
red, ocher, bronze, gold. The lawn littered with a glowing detritus.

And now the cold winds at midday,
                         scattered showers,
dead leaves blowing from the maples, the sky socked in at night.
A lone jetliner rumbles overhead under cloudcover,
rain pattering at the grape's canopy of leaves,

the hail-battered lettuce beds, the sky a smoky glass,

                                        winter coming.

                              *

In our bed we've shared
                    more years than not, cocooned in down
we listen to the ancient elm pair at the end of the block
strain in the night, their great sinewed trunks
                                        grown old, battered,
their thick bark lichen-flecked, balding.
Some wayward lower limbs too heavy and horizontal,
                    weak crotches, you call them —
better to be cut away clean,
                    then left to tear away ragged
in the next winter storm, splitting the trunk.

The long, dolorous cry of a Burlington Northern train
pierces the darkness,
                    less warning than song,
fading as it disappears into a tunnel under the city.
                              Siren of the lost and the looking.
Though for years we've searched by light of day
we've never found
                    where the tunnel emerges.

                              *

A cloud of starlings swarms the twin cathedral steeples
of St. James, beautiful in the long angled light,
circling and sweeping
                    the giant flock a creature of one
undecided mind: wheeling under the high clouds
as the sun begins to fall
                    a flurry of landing and taking off again,
like an amoeba, splitting and coming back together,
spreading out to fill the sky, and then contracting to a point.

As night descends, they are gone,
to roost in the dark bare trees, to sleep.

*

Season of sedge and reed, catkin and berry.

A patch of sunlight breaks through the gray,
                              retouching the maples
with a brandy-colored light.

The grape on its pergola, twin vines arching.
Leaves redder than ever before.

Serafina

That day the sky seemed torn open like a letter.
All morning on the television bodies falling

in flames as steel and glass towers crumbled.
Unable to look any longer, my partner and I

wandered the late summer garden —
the kniphofia in tatters, a few pears

bruised and fallen near the birdbath,
our own city shining and intact in the distance,

but the sky eerily quiet, not a plane,
not a bird in sight.

Come evening we walked
to the neighborhood bistro. How oddly

soothing to watch the hostess guide us
to our favorite table, offer us menus, fill our glasses

with iced water — her movements calm and assured,
as if nothing astonishing had happened.

How the votive candle's gentle flickering
lit my partner's face, and the bread and the oil

the waiter brought seemed almost sacramental.
The makeshift stage doubling as storage

for table linens and crates of wine
created a kind of glorious rubble.

The amateur singer, nervous but beautiful
atop her high stool, nodded to the piano player

before beginning her first notes
cautiously, carefully. They played

a bluesy jazz from another era, mysterious
but familiar in its tumbling melody,

her smoky voice and his answering piano
the well-worn strands of an engagement

between lovers. As they seamlessly finished
each other's lines I remembered

how that other couple stood
together on their fiery ledge —

how they turned to each other and
joined hands, before stepping off.

Aeschylus in the Park

Hot summer evening — blanket spread
upon the outdoor theater's wide lawn,
a text two thousand years old
summoned to life by the barest of props:
cement stage, draped tunic, voice.

We watch the cycle of curses
and killings unfold — children
slaughtered and fed to their parents,
a daughter sacrificed to indifferent
gods, the mother scheming
to murder her murdering husband.

Across the centuries Electra's grief
rages fresh as a wound.
We imagine ourselves noble,
but this need for vengeance is ancient
as the evening sun
now thinning to a blade over the city.

The plot continues its downward spiral.
The night sky grows cool and full of stars.
Is this how we light the darkness,
with our meager words,
our feeble human torches?

Night Walk

Haystack Rock, Cannon Beach, Oregon

Guesthouse lamps glimmer in the distance
as we hike the beach on bare feet,
sand like wet clay between our toes,
the evening's blue dome perforated with stars.

Slowly, the great coastal lith rises like a fortress,
crumbling bedrock exposed by retreating
ocean, its gleaming tidepools
dark with starfish and anemones.

Humbled by the rock's colossal shadow, we watch
the summer constellations turn on their axis, listen
to distant breakers cresting far beyond
this wide strand littered with broken shells and kelp.

Out there, you say, pointing
to the luminous white hush at the horizon.
I want my ashes out there.

You're not dying any more than I am
or any of us is — still a sadness washes over me.

A hermit crab sweeps up on shore,
pincers opening and closing around air.
How it claws for its small life,
the endlessly departing sea.

NOTES

The opening line of "Tête-à-tête" is borrowed from Christina Georgina Rossetti's poem "A Birthday."

"The Devil's Dictionary of Medical Terms" comprises anagrams of common medical terms.

"Lost in Translation" owes a debt to AltaVista's online Babel Fish Translation program.

"Fugue" was culled from random text produced from three of William Carlos Williams's short poems entered into a Markov text generator.

"Nursemaid's Elbow" refers to a partial dislocation of the elbow, caused by a sudden pull on a child's arm or hand. It is for Kathleen Flenniken.

"Crossing the Pear" owes a debt to Victor Perera's fascinating book about the Pereira/Perera family name, and the Portuguese-Jewish diaspora, *The Cross and the Pear Tree: A Sephardic Journey*. Pereira means pear tree in Portuguese.

The two stanzas of "Doppelgänger" contain exactly the same words, rearranged. The first stanza recounts the day Dean and I met in 1986; the second refers to the same day, twenty years later.

Peter Pereira is a family physician at High Point Community
Clinic in West Seattle, where he takes care of an urban, under-
served population of refugees, immigrants, housing project resi-
dents, young families, and the elderly. Many of his poems arise
from his medical practice, and have appeared in *Poetry, Prairie
Schooner, New England Review, Journal of the American Medical
Association,* and elsewhere. He has presented on the subject of
Poetry & Medicine at medical schools and writing conferences
across the country. His books include *The Lost Twin* (Grey Spider,
2000) and *Saying the World* (Copper Canyon, 2003), which won
the Hayden Carruth Award and was a finalist for the Lambda
Literary Award, the Triangle Publishing Award, and the PEN West
Award. He lives in Seattle with his partner, Dean Allan.

The Chinese character for poetry is made up of two parts: "word" and "temple." It also serves as pressmark for Copper Canyon Press.

Since 1972, Copper Canyon Press has fostered the work of emerging, established, and world-renowned poets for an expanding audience. The Press thrives with the generous patronage of readers, writers, booksellers, librarians, teachers, students, and funders—everyone who shares the belief that poetry is vital to language and living.

Major funding has been provided by:
Anonymous (2)
The Paul G. Allen Family Foundation
Lannan Foundation
National Endowment for the Arts
Washington State Arts Commission

For information and catalogs:
COPPER CANYON PRESS
Post Office Box 271
Port Townsend, Washington 98368
360-385-4925
www.coppercanyonpress.org

THE **PAUL G. ALLEN** **FAMILY** *foundation*

Lannan

NATIONAL ENDOWMENT FOR THE ARTS

This book was designed and typeset by Phil Kovacevich, using Minion for the text and Avenir for the titles. Minion was designed for Adobe Systems in 1989 by Robert Slimbach. Minion is inspired by classical, old-style typefaces of the late Renaissance, a period of elegant, beautiful, and highly readable type designs. Avenir was designed by Adrian Frutiger and released by Linotype-Hell in 1988. The design is based on two earlier sanserif typefaces, Erbar and Futura. Printed by McNaughton & Gunn.